MW01480484

Praise for *Little Fish*

"Memory and myth work in tandem in Sylvia Fox's *Little Fish*, as fantastical creatures are conjured to explore family history, and ghosts serve as reminders. Fox asks us, how are we to make sense of the stories we've inherited—whether we wanted them or not?"

– Jonah Barnett, filmmaker and author of *Moss-Covered Claws*

"*Little Fish* is a beautiful and sacred experience. The story, the words, the images...they rock you from fever dreams to lullabies, from anger and deep wounds to healing through the ancient magic of spirit and nature. It should be savored, taken in slow and more than once...like you would a prayer. You will do well to fall into Sylvia Fox's spell – there is movement and wonder as well as the gift of learning and being blessed by ancestral wisdom. Most importantly, the reader will experience the very special connection to the complex, but global pursuit of women working to heal through generations, past time and trauma, to infinite love and liberation. It is potent, a unique exploration of the bloody, beautiful mysteries of life."

– Kellie Richardson, author of *The Art of Naming My Pain*, *What Us Is*, and former City of Tacoma Poet Laureate

"A dizzying epic that circles around generational history, *Little Fish* remembers, forgets, and revives familial narratives through a splendor of mythology, oral histories, and glimpses into the present moment. Among the mesmerizing hums of Brazilian figures are entangling twines of motherhood and left-behind fragments of reincarnated women. Fox expertly brings about magic with every line and footnote, inviting the reader to listen to each ghost while simultaneously pushing them to the margins if they ever attempt to understand the secrets that do not belong to them. *Little Fish* honors our own bodies' history, and how generational cycles are repeated, questioned, and expanded to create a new legacy built upon ancestral knowledge."

– Alissa Tu, author of *Confessions of a Modern Day Kumiho*

A sonorous, female-led epic of lineage, loss, and belonging—women adrift in grief so deep it threatens to swallow them. This is the Odyssey the 21st century needs: set on Brazilian waters, steeped in African and Native Brazilian deities, and written with a linguistic precision that will leave readers spellbound.

– Flavia Stefani, writer and translator

LITTLE FISH

Sylvia Fox

Blue Cactus Press | caləɬali

ʔuk'ʷədiid čəɬ ʔuhigʷəd txʷəl tiiɬ ʔa čəɬ ʔal tə swatxʷixʷtxʷəd ʔə tiiɬ puyaləpabš. ʔa ti dxʷʔa ti swatxʷixʷtxʷəd ʔə tiiɬ puyaləpabš ʔəsɬaɬaƛ̕lil tul'al tudiʔ tuhaʔkʷ. didiʔɬ ʔa həlgʷəʔ ʔal ti sləx̌il. dxʷəsɬaƛ̕lils həlgʷəʔ gʷəl ƛ̕'uyayus həlgʷəʔ gʷəl ƛ̕'uƛ̕'ax̌ʷad həlgʷəʔ tiiɬ bədədəʔs gʷəl tix̌dxʷ həlgʷəʔ tiiɬ ʔiišəds həlgʷəʔ gʷəl ƛ̕'uʔalalus həlgʷəʔ gʷəl ƛ̕'utxʷəlšucidəb. x̌ʷəla··b ʔə tiiɬ tuyəl'yəlabs.

Blue Cactus Press is located in caləɬali, on puyaləpabš land. This land was stolen and colaonized by settlers via the signing of the Treaty of Medicine Creek in 1854. Since then, it has not been returned to its rightful and traditional stewards, puyaləpabš, also known as the Puyallup Tribe of Indians.

We acknowledge that we benefit from our existence at caləɬali. And we are thankful to live, work, and be in relationship with the land and people here.

Table of Contents

I

My belly distends now.
The shadows swell,
sunlight soft as ceremony.
The shadows hold the shape
of *Pernambuco*.[1]
But shadows do not speak.
Their hearts are not red.
They cannot tell me stories
of any coast, of *saudade*.[2]

Waves distort the shadows
into aunties and mothers,
indeed, giving them a voice.

1 Also called Brazilwood, *pau-brasil*, and, in Tupi, *ibirapitanga*. A red dye can be made from soaking the wood. It is said that this is where the name "Brazil" comes from, land of Brazilwood, but there are older stories with forgotten names by people who knew this land better, and newer stories by coastal women who mourn the loss of that wild wooded welcome.

2 A lyrical kind of yearnng or nostalgia. Feel it in your cheeks, roll it across your tongue, *sau-da-de*.

You dream me into memory,
which tastes like iron.
"*Mãmae*[3] was part of me, *Yemanjá*.[4]
"Why wouldn't she be kin to you?"
"I don't know,
but I dreamed her dreams, my mother's."
There are questions that
I still need answered.
"Why wouldn't she be kin to you?"
asks Yemanjá.
"A mother's stories are
her daughter's womb.
She made you, didn't she?
Why wouldn't she be kin to you?"
"No. Deeper than that," I say.
"Where can I start?
I didn't need to wake
my mother at dawn to ask,
Were these your dreams or mine?
Memory tastes like metal, brined.
I've learned to recognize it.
I haven't dreamed for years, and now
I grow a little fish and
dream again, the taste of tears."
"I understand saltwater better than most,"
she replies.

3 *Mãe* and *Mamãe* are both used to identify "mother," similar to Mom, Mommy, Mother, any other word you use to yearn for the womb you knew before this one.

4 Goddess of the ocean, or generally of water and water ways, sometimes associated with fertility, the "mother," in the Afro-Brazilian mystic tradition of Candomblé. There are many visual representations of some amalgamation of this figure and the mother Mary from the catholic tradition. Imagine floating, tide pools, salt water caves, sea storms, tsunamis, drowning. Just think of the sea, just feel how she knows you.

"When Mãe and I were sleeping,
we dreamed a pink dolphin[5], the
shadow of the pink dolphin,
because he came always in disguise.
In the dream our eyes were shut
beneath the shadow of the dolphin,
who had disguised itself as my mother's brother,
it was becoming her brother;
it would forever be her brother.
But still it had the smell
of rivers, and the ocean,
the sea slick skin of legends
and ancient history, hungry.
She and I were one, in bed,
with both our eyes shut until
he left us,
wishing him to leave us.
He was there to take her from me,
don't you see?"

5 There are many versions of this mythological figure from the Amazon, a pink dolphin in the rivers thought to be able to transform itself into a man, sometimes disguising the hump on its head under a hat. There are many warnings associated with the pink dolphin, mainly that he transforms into a man who seeks to attract and then take advantage of women. It has been, perhaps, a story to talk about sexual assault.

"Mãe?"
Menina.[6]

We lie in your bed, floating in an ocean,
our arms stretching for each coast,
to stay afloat, Mãe.

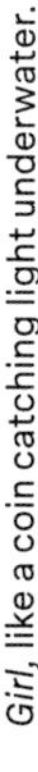
6 *Girl*, like a coin catching light underwater.

A water goddess is circulating
rip tides and whirlpools and droughts.

We woke with our hands in the ocean,
and licked the salt from our fingertips,
not knowing what it was for.
And I saw us becoming ocean, Mãe,
uprush, backrush, high tide, riptide,
we were becoming a tsunami over the whole
of Salvador,
of Bahia,
of Brazil.[7]

7 Salvador, short for São Salvador da Bahia de Todos os Santos (Holy Savior of the Bay of All Saints) is the capital city of the Brazilian state of Bahia. It served as a critical port city for slave trade in the Americas, and it was the site of the first slave market in "the New World," home to many ghosts.

Yemanjá, sea goddess—
goddess of water—
her voice bubbles up in a whisper in my ear,
and it seems that you look out
from my eyes, Mãe.[8]
She speaks in water,
rippling, white noise, surf, spray,
waves come from her mouth
and there is no translation for it.

“Do you have a daughter?” she asks
in Portuguese and Yoruba.
Yes, Flor. You know her.
“That is right. A woman like you
deserves to have a daughter. One who’s
been through what you’ve been through
should have a daughter on her chest.”
Where is she? I took her away from everyone,
and further. Who could I trust? A pink dolphin
found us off the Gulf of Mexico.
Won’t they ever leave us alone?
Won’t he ever leave me?
Did you not see my daughter
when you found me?
Water is our family tree, Mãe,
its roots are in rivers, streams, bedrock.
We grow redhearted brazilwood

8 Depending on which syncretic traditions bring you to the Orixás, possession is a common way they deliver messages. Possession by mothers’ ghosts, however, does not require Orixás.

far from home, with roots to the
Brazilian city on the sea.

I tried to show you how the cobblestone of
your dreams were the same as in that town
that we called home together,
here and there, then and now.
I visited the magic store man for cures for
missing forks, whispering boards, gnarled
trees that hid the body of a Kiowa chief,
haunting far from home[9], old and gnarled.
Trees hide so many secrets.

Yemanjá, water spirit, floats nearby,
singing the tide into my hands,
making my palms into cupped paddles.
She is not confused by the waves,
and so I've asked her for answers.
But she says I am the one with the answers.
She is everywhere, as if
the water of the Atlantic Ocean
hangs too in the humid Texas summer air—
as if heat waves
could conjure the sea.

9 This is one ghost, but you have your own. Just look for "helped" and "asked for" in the history books. Either way, they say Chief Spotted Tail was buried horizontally.

The question wells up from a deep place,
somewhere I had almost forgotten.
What happened to my mother? I ask her,
but she responds only in dreams.
At night, a full moon—
the way I remember it,
smoke rising from the neighbor's bonfire,
I twitch like spirits or moths, wondering,
when I find you, which home we might return to—
the water of the whole earth running in my veins.

We were always soaking in the swimming pool,
always Texas summer nights, bright and warm,
always the ticking of insects and
the moon marking time, waxing, full, waning,
fingernail moon hanging from the sky.

When you finally brought me to your hometown,
my grandmother's house was like ours,
like coyotes howling night
as they passed beneath the window,
floating in the swimming pool at night where
I could feel eyes though I couldn't see them.

I am on cobblestone again dreaming.
The men whistle and grope.
My Havaiana rubber slaps back against the stone.
The moisture in the sea air dampens everything.
My sandals slap up against the soles of my feet
and wake me. There you are beside me,
there you are on the ceiling above me.
"Did you eat my father?" I ask.
The air outside is heavy with moisture.
Blink, from a dozen eyes.
Like the devout mantis, some spiders eat their mates.
You look at me from so many eyes,
I wonder if you haven't always been arachnid.
"Where is my father!"
When I shout, you skitter back
into whatever corner you came from,
leaving me more alone.
You are beside me, waking.
You never saw the spider.
There are no men here,
just the ghost of my unborn brother
who sits at the edge of the bed.
I don't remember what I asked for.
Yemanjá floats me downy leaves from
the magnolia tree, sends me flowers,
thick, magnolia air.

"Who are you to me?
Who are you to me, to my mother?"
She steadies my billowing hair with a wet hand.
Takes an oil smelling of seaweed to my scalp.
Many ghostly eyes are bobbing in the surf.

"The women I keep company with here dove
willingly from off the decks of ships," she says,
and then sings a soothing current
as she braids, as if I knew
her ocean tongue.
"I am *axé*.[10] I am every ocean,
every sea—
the pink dolphin is my family, too.
Who am I to mothers and
to daughters?
Who am I to you?
I cannot give you answers,
though sometimes I have been answers
whispered in ship hulls
and shackles.
But you, you must go on the long journey for
answers yourself—
through family and time.
You must leach the memories
inherited in blood...
The cicadas signal summer, May or June...

10 *Axé* could mean a lot of things — the spirit, the life force, an energy, a type of music, something you can harness in *capoeira*, sacred energy of the *orixás* in candomblé.

Your name is Flor, and you are barely
six or seven...
You like to find the thin, shed shell
cicada skins that cling to trees...
You like the smell of Tia
boiling slime off the okra on the stove...
some incantations...
You know your ancestors
by their mask carvings
hanging from the wall, wooden faces lined in stories,
warrior, hunter, earth mother, healer,
I, Yemanjá...

I like to keep company
with stories.
I am a guide.
I like stories for their currents.
I like to see a girl who can draw story
from an unfamiliar shape.
I am current, *o vai e vem*, the coming and going.
So I emerged like you from brush,
was spoken from the split mouth of the earth
while a mourning dove sang in her sleep.
I emerged from watery, seasick hips,
from a rhythm carried across the ocean.

I was yanked by my long hair, and later
reborn amidst a rebel army,
and born amidst the first new world
market of bodies,
and born at the last siege of Palmares,
that old *quilombo*,
and born on the ink of ancestral land rights
written over in blood—
by the trickster. Who else?
Do you remember that hot rain of summer?"
"Yes—"
"Saci[11] is in the sky, making trouble.
He grabs the tails of clouds
and whips them overhead, wind and rain,
heading north, heavy with oceans and
spirits who have all but been forgotten.
As naturally as coyotes
howling night across the dried-out
creek bed— Saci.
You remember the storms,
that humid Texas summer of the talking moon,
filled with ghosts.
Is this your aunt's *otá*?[12]
Her sacred stone?"
"Yes—"
"Imprinted in seashells. Its own
mind, voice, gift.
Its colors are a language, too.

11 The trickster of Brazilian folklore, a young, one-legged boy who smokes a pipe, wears a magical cap, and inspires fear. He is a "dark-skinned" boy in the stories. Although this figure seems to have originated in Tupi tradition, its appropriation into the "Brazilian" identity may have roots in slavery and racism.

12 The *Otá* is a sacred stone, an honored object within someone's private candomblé shrine. The stone would be kept hidden, unseen, but "fed" with various objects and elements around it. A person would associate their stone with a particular deity, and it's believed to contain the *axé*, or life force, of that deity. An *otá* finds you, not the other way around. The article "The Hidden Life of Stones: Historicity, Materiality and the Value of Candomblé Objects in Bahia," gives a longer reflection on these stones.

See how the black shines blue
and green under the water?
The colors of returning home.
Shined in the oil from your palm.
This stone was your aunt's,
but it called to you.
I call you, but you must grow
the stone yourself..."
She applies shimmering oils to my
skin next, smelling of coconuts and
palms, as if to summon the night sky,
the full moon, the passing clouds.
I grow the stone. I grow the universe
across my skin.
Her cryptic phrases become current again,
ocean rhythm.
The full moon winks me into backyard swimming pools,
pools which are echoes of sky across fields of tall grasses.
Mãe and Tia sink their feet deep,
while I float in circles or reach, unthinking, for the edge,
to crack loose tiles from their porous crowns.
We spend long evenings soaking in chlorine,
as the neighbor's smoke drifts overhead
like spirits. Summer storms are coming, transforming
swimming pools into ocean,
backyards into ocean,
horizons into ocean.
"I can't remember taking the stone."

"You almost never can.
That's the trouble with *otás*. They are living.
They choose you.
This *otá* is very old."

This is a peaceful place,
except for the eyes.
I saw the dolphin again, Mãe.
The same.
It was not so fearsome as before,
a ghost of a dolphin, its eyes glazed over,

spinning the water, confused
amidst so many eyes,
lost and split,
its pale pink skin a mess of puckered scars.

When I was a little girl,
the pink dolphin came by rivers and streams
from the Amazon to our city on the bay,
disguised as my eldest brother.
He comes at night, Boto-cor-de-Rosa.[13]
He comes by water, by disguise,
by fathers and mothers and brothers
and ghosts.

Do you remember your finger on the wet horizon?
You told me there were signs
and locked the windows.
Ghosts come at night.
They come by water, come disguised.

Tia Malu nods in agreement as you tell the story.
She nods before you've finished,
as if to interrupt you,
yes yes yes,
she nods and says,

13 Another name for the pink dolphin of legends, percussive, like a drum or stones or gunshots.

14 Play on Portuguese words for "crazy".

"The pink dolphin will come.
He's come before.
He's always coming.
We'll be ready."
Tia Malu, Tia Lulu, Tia Maluca,[14]
she believed that if you mixed together
the right oils for forgetting,
you could forget.
She dreamed up signs.
She dreamed only of the future.
Now, looking back, I can see
the distrust bloom between you,
you, desperate for truth or lessons
from the past, she, desperate to leave the past
for new truths.

"Acorda, Mãe—"
ãinn...[15]

The eyes are growing teeth.

I dream the tentacle of your voice
wrapping around my ankle,
pulling me underwater.
Long, thick stalks of endless kelp.

15 "Wake up, Mãe—" or maybe "Come back to me—".

16 In some versions of the story of the pink dolphin, the dolphin holds secret knowledge. The local doctor or spiritual leader would go deep into the water to discover the hidden underwater city with a name like *Encante* or no name at all, where they might learn something of the pink dolphin's secret knowledge to bring back to the village.

Encante,[16] your voice teases
as shadow and light twist my chest.
You are gone, leaving me with the name
of that underwater paradise,
a shifting seabed, the pink dolphin circling.
How do you trap me here?
How even gone do you trap me?
I whet my shells and stone, keep them sharp;
keep the past from growing.

We saw the ghost on the wet horizon.
We stalked through grass.
We bathed in it.
We knew only currents bringing storms
from an el niño summer.
We knew only currents bringing purple skies,
green skies, skies heavy with the Gulf,
and you, strong like *Avó*,
you my grandmother's daughter,
you were ready to cut down oceans.

Yemanjá grinds shells into powder.[17]
She calls on elders.

I remember my grandmother's scaled hands,

17 Rituals, always rituals. Have you asked for permission to read these stories, to speak with ghosts, to enter the sea? *Pedir licença*, in all practices of magic or living.

She showed me how her scales reflected moonlight,
shimmered rage, lament,
and how they stunned,
and she would cut down other fish
as they swam past.
She too prayed to oceans.
She was fish,
stronger, harder, meaner when she had to be,
killing other fish when she had to.
When I dream her,
I read the story back to her
where she beat it on your skin.
It's only natural, she tells me.
A fish births other fish,
dolphins, sirens, stars,
and we repeat the motions, all of us
float away on boats,
inherit water.
I wrap my own arms around me, you,
with seashells for my hair.
Yemanjá is pulling masked faces
from the sea.
Wants me to repeat the chant
she calls out for memory:
saudade saudade saudade

One wall was always wrapped in masks.
I used to listen, my ear pressed to the
wooden faces, suspended
hollow eyes, lips like mine,
soft jaws, for whispers of a home
where history crests the earth
on roots, history,
deep inland, riverside,
popped from red *guaraná* eyes,[18]
dark woman in a dark forest with
history dribbling from her lips—

I am descended from Africans and Natives both,
runners, vines, waterways, tide,
my story, pushing, pulling, back.

"What do you see now, Flor?"
asks the water spirit.
"My grandmother shimmering
as she moves through water,
the way I shimmer now.
She sharpens a shell from a bed
of sand or seaweed
and cuts a bloody circle around her body,
the shell pointed in, cutting her own torso,
out, bleeding the fish around her,

18 In one version of the myth of the Guaraná plant, after a child was killed by a deity, a different deity took one of the child's eyes and planted it, from which the Guaraná grew. The fruit shows a resemblance to eyes.

then she tucks the shell away,
her scales shimmering."

My mother took with her the heavy carvings
of my ancestors, hid them for me,
so I'd know my peoples' faces,
small, striking, laden, filled a wall with them.
I am descended from Africans and Natives.

I've forgotten how the women in my family
worked magic,
that Tia's closet is filled with boxes,
and smells like a burning bush.
I lie on her bed with my head tipped back,
catching sight of bottles, grasses, shells,
cloths, beads
refracting and reflecting sunlight.[19]
I close my eyes.

When I open them,
my head dipped back,
I'm looking up to the moon.
"I thought it was daytime,
daylight."
These are dreams.

19 If you don't know how to use these objects for magic, I won't tell you, not now. You don't understand me yet, but you will.

I've swallowed the sun.
I touch the melon of your belly.
All right. Moon then.
You and I, side by side.
The water tongues my temples,
tastes me. I can't move.
"Mãe—
I'm scared, Mãe."
You aren't here.
"I'm scared."
I strain against the rising tide,
something, someone, holding me.
"Memories are like the tides.

This ocean is vast,
moon drawing from it memories
as you float," says Yemanjá,
her fingers on my temples.
"Where have you been, Mãe?"
"What do you mean, girl?"
"I felt my mother near me, I heard her voice.
I turned and she was trying to ask me something."
I taste salt.
My mouth is full of it.
"What is it you think you could give her?"
"There are all the things I wish I could have been.
I want to change the story,

to maroon us on a desert, where water
spills only from the mouths of flowers,
where our skins could harden into leather.
I would have us dry out so completely
that even the moon would be powerless.
She should never have been alone."

Flor—flowering pernambuco eyes,
treebark skin, red, home.
I want to take the skin off that girl,
crawl underneath it, take it.

"Did you hear her?"
She floats there, all eyes,
hungry, you hear her?
And then as if she's given up,
she ducks and disappears into the ocean.
"Mãe, why are you thrashing the water like that?
What do you need? Stay still a moment.
Give me your hands. Or— listen—"
"You can't reach her that way."
"What way?"
"Those aren't the words."
And what if I crawl into the refuge of her skin—

The womb of the woman who made
herself my home,
who put me in between worlds.
Together we made a new world.

She seeks out my breasts like an infant, I the mother,
but I have nothing for her there, only skin, blood,
the two of us grown women.
"How did you find me, Mãe?"
You might have come with me,
there's ocean for anyone.
"Enough ocean to lose you—?"
She gives up the suckling.
I've had enough of oceans.
You might have come for me earlier.
Ask me to, minha Florzinha.[20]
Ask me to stay.
"Of course—"
Ask me to stay—
But I taste salt, at the back of my throat there.
The words won't come. I can't speak those words.
Are you scared?
I want to make a home in the sand for us,
a place to blow from dune to dune.
My voice returned, I ask,
"Has it always been this way, Mãe?"
How?

20 A pet name, "my little flower".

"Between mothers and daughters."
Yes.
In the desert, we won't feel ourselves moved
by the phases of the moon.
We won't feel tides well within us,
and you won't leave me, Mãe,
and there will be no distance between us.
We drove a long way,
yellow stretching out from all sides,
and she said I should sleep,
could sleep, now
she knew how to lose ghosts.
Texas had sunsets that stretched into eternity.

"I'm scared, Mãe."
"What, girl?"
"Something isn't right."
You must know what it is.
"Something happens here,
I don't know.
You made this drive alone.
The skies are purple-green,
this isn't the time for oceans.
We shouldn't be going."
"You have only to float,"
says Yemanjá.
"Why are you afraid?"

Quiet, Flor.
Your eyes are pink where they should be white,
flecked with black like flies.
I haven't dreamed for years, and now
I dream, again, the taste of tears,
the sound of the Bradford Pear tree
scraping against my bedroom window,
its branches fast growing but weak,
casting shadows, sounds, snapping.
"Remember, you used to check every corner
of the bedroom so I wouldn't be afraid?
When I said there and there and
there and there too,
you checked them all.
Why not now?
Was it because you felt the fear yourself then?
And because then you wanted to put mine with yours,
so that they'd find courage in each other?"
You used to take me.
We crossed the bridge to coastline.
We parked up in the dunes at the edge of the island,
you and me.
Like home, you said.
The ocean was your home,
more than your home.
The ocean was your rhythm, your tempo.
You would float for hours
when home wasn't enough.

"Can we go home?" I asked.
You looked empty then, or
full of longing. You closed your eyes,
baptized yourself, head underwater.
We'd been gone for days,
staying at some bayside motel that
smelled of chlorine, sunscreen, cigarettes.
I didn't know what you were planning,
I wanted to get back.
"Take me home," I said again,
over and over, seaside, poolside, in the room,
in the bed we shared, you with your nightmares.
"Take me home—"
And when I finally awoke to you,
not in your beach wrap, but clothed and pulling bags,
I felt relieved. As if there was some danger in staying here.
I had no words for it then.
You didn't once mention ghosts
on the long drive home.
And on returning, there I was,
again, in the yard, chasing cricket sounds,
thinking it was over.
Would I have pleaded, have let you take me home,
had I known that you'd return to that place
all on your own?

"I saw him, my uncle, while he lived,
all of us staying in my grandmother's house.
We went out for the boardwalk artists,
for the man with the machete slashing coconuts,
the frenetic energy of beachside musicians,
people playing along, barside, slapping thighs,
tabletops, shoulders, bare feet slapping pavement
in the dance. The steps: twist, back back fore,
twist, the steps, at home,
lock the door until morning,
I saw my uncle there, in my grandmother's house, drinking."

You remember that night before the storms?
you ask me, as we float on this timeless raft. I correct you,
"The storms had already begun,"
as if time wasn't the current, this mass of ocean,
there and there and
there and there, too, all at once.
Sometimes I can't remember
if I love you or I hate you,
you who are my mother,
you, taking her away.

"She loved you."
"Yes, I've told you that."
"You were there for her."

"I hope not only for being there—
I'm her daughter. She's my mother.
Isn't that reason enough?"
"Does that make you feel better?"
"Yes."
"You were her daughter,
what does it matter?"
"Because it matters."

The shadows, Flor. Look at the shadows—
But I held your face and looked only at your eyes,
your eyelashes gatekeeping your grief.

Back home, the nightmares were gone.
You slept in silence, and
I knew only relief, floating,
the moon as a shadow.
Do you see her? you asked me.
I ignored the question.
You asked again, hypnotized
by your own doubling,
the copy of you there, hovering,
close to the ceiling.
"No," I lied, refusing to look up.

I want to be held by her again.
I want her to hold me.
I want her strong enough to hold me.
I want not to feel so alone
What is the reason we find ourselves
in all this water?

“Who wrote the stories so that
they changed with every telling?
New lessons and new mothers, every time,
at least a dozen likenesses and nothing I can trust.
Who wrote the stories this way?
You are the ancient one,
tell me, what among the old stories is true?”
“Is not the entire ocean true?”
“I’m not asking after oceans—”
“Aren’t you?”

Mãe yawns or makes a brief and
silent scream,
her teeth shine back the light
reflecting off the water where she floats.
I try to remember whether ghosts have teeth,
or if she might be something else entirely.
She’s been gone such a long time now.

Sometimes in dreams the spirit
who has entered you is a woman.[21]
A ghost follows your scent,
stows herself away in the cook's quarters
on a ship,
like you did,
crosses oceans to meet you,
floods her way in on a technicolor storm.

Sometimes the ghost hides herself
in a photograph,
bides her time in Tia's cluttered closet,
amidst the shrine of spirit magic,
gathering strength with dust, waiting
for a troublemaking trickster to lure
a curious girl,
then sets herself atop my ribcage and
pushes her way in. Or

sometimes she appears on the horizon
as a heat wave, floats the waves of summer heat,
dances along cicada wings,
rises with the morning humidity,
comes into view at the edge
of the yard,
walks right up to the front door,

21 A body can be entered by a spirit for any number of reasons. If someone begins to act strangely, it might be that a spirit has entered them and is causing trouble.

takes her cafezinho in the kitchen with you—
familiar to you—
disappears only to meet me in the garden shed,
grasps my bottom jaw and crawls down my throat
to set herself inside my chest.
The ghost is in me.
The ghost who knows you.

The night before, during, or after the storms,
we jumped into, floated in, or splashed around
a swimming pool, the pool hardly holding its shape,
lined or not so lined in tiles, its concrete flaking,
the yard cracking, tectonic plates shifting,
the neighbor's fire smoking,
the sky trembling, weeping, still,
the whole earth threatening to tear itself open
and swallow,
and we, inside a concrete swimming pool
you and me and Tia,
or you and me and Tia and a set of two reflective eyes
at the edge of the yard,
an uncle or a ghost or a ghost of an uncle, all of us
in or out of water—

"What are you thinking, Flor?"
asked the spirit who steadied
rivers, lakes, the sea.

"Tia is running the bath.
She tells me there are no dolphins here,
that they are only stories
trapped in dreams.
Tia is saying Mãe will have to
find her own way back to us,
that no one can go to where she is going."
But there are ghosts in the bathwater,
and she is alone.

Sometimes I imagine a door,
you, slipping through it,
into shadow.
Sometimes it is that simple.

It's easy to imagine you'll come back.

"Your mother dwells on things she should be forgetting."
Tia Malu smells like cigarettes.
She hates to smell like cigarettes,

so she holds her hand away from the rest of her body, as if
it is separate from her, as if her hand floats,
disconnected from her body, feeding her cigarettes.
The smoke makes me calm, dizzy, forgetful.

I stay away for one moment and
surely it is in that moment something
creeps in through the bathwater and sets itself
to work there in your ribcage.

You call out for me.
Flor—
"I'm here, Mãe, I'm here."

You are stalked by a shadow self.
I lie beside you, my heart in my mouth,
my eyes closed. My body is frozen
as yours skitters this way and that along the ceiling,
maybe contending with my refusal to see you,
or maybe with my brother's ghost at the foot of the bed,
who comes from the same world of
shadow selves, of selves choked out.
I can hear the sounds of fingernails above us,
quiet as we are.

I'm thinking now of brothers,
of my brother's ghost who never ages,
of boys who don't grow into men,
and whether mothers are more afraid
of boys dying young
or boys becoming men,
and what do mothers think of daughters then?
Are we not also fearful?

In my dreams, Mãe, you're the little turtle,
Jabutí, *Jabuta*, *Jabuticaba*, all tricks and
games, tucking yourself into the belly
of Eagle's guitar.[22]

22 Jabutí is a folkloric turtle trickster. In one story, the turtle climbed into Eagle's guitar for a party (in some versions, Eagle tricked Jabutí into getting into the guitar, as payback for the turtle's tricks). Eventually, Jabutí falls from high in the sky, and the animals help put the shell back together, leaving the lines in the turtle's shell.

You are the eyes disappearing into clouds.
In my dream, you're a turtle, and
Eagle plucks you, tucks you into his guitar
and takes you away into clouds.

Will you go back with me?
"No, Mãe."
I'm afraid that the ocean will swallow you,
but if I refuse to go, you won't go either.
I believe it still,
despite the full moon's pull
that gives even the bathwater a tide,
that makes your body sway,
so full with water.
In my dreams, you're a guitar belly
on Eagle's back, splashing
salt water, dripping sky into my mouth,
splashing, dripping, falling out, swallowed, gone.

"You know that the pink dolphin is more than the stories,
you know that stories cannot be trapped inside of dreams."
"Yes. I know the story.
I always wait and wait and wait,
I know the story, but
I wait to see her falling through the air
from unimaginable heights.
I can see the shell shatter
before she hits the ground."
"That isn't the way it happens."
"Yes, but in the dream—"

Where do you go when the mothers are gone?
My belly grows the way my mother's belly grew.
"Who did this to you?"
"A sweet and gentle man. If Mãe were here, I'd tell her
I had a sweet man, gentle,
the kind of man she didn't believe in."
"He's gone now?"
"Yes."
"Where is your mother, your aunt?"
"Gone, gone. They're all gone. This, now,
this quiet between tenderness and birth
is where death resides,
loneliness, death, a home.
I didn't breathe for months, you know, waiting
after I lost him, too.

No, not waiting, not anything,
a time with no air where nothing happened.
I must have died there. My body isn't mine.
A body moved one morning, done with waiting,
sat in a car, and drove to anything, south, from anywhere,
the way my mother used to journey."

I try to hold you, but you find it silly,
daughter holding mother.
This is how you hold me instead,
with snakes in the garden to wrap me,
yes, roots, to hold me, your arms,
I lie with you and sleep
amongst the thick yucca leaves,
okra like a weed, and *couve,* greens,
I lie and eat and dream.

Our story starts before me,
the magic in your dreams
an old magic, from blood.
There have been others,
mothers, daughters,
to lie around sharing dreams,
to writhe in sand, or
cut skin amongst the kinds of
thickets that haunt riversides,

the undersides of *mata ciliar*,[23]
dreaming, kicking up old memories,
becoming tide.
Long before I confessed to you
all that I could see, you shared images
in dreams, and I knew everything,
(even without incantations or wombs,
there is always dream magic),
and we traveled far.

In those dreams, the full moon spoke
nostalgia, sighed with pleasure,
shimmered over young nights of
Bahia's carnival, painted across stars
the boys who donned their mothers'
and their sisters' dresses,
flashing hems in the breeze,
their chests filled with fruit,
the glitter of gods swinging from dancers' hips,
dancers squeezing themselves, their bodies.
Drums, as if the rhythms
lifted off the streets themselves,
the chests of people, elbows, dancers
popping up and down and up.
This, too, was life.

23 Portuguese word for Riparian forest, the forested area of land adjacent to a body of water.

We could have lived endlessly in those dreams.

This is the way it was, Mãe,
when I lay beside you and
you made me dream your dreams.
Dreams from some life you had lived.
I let my arms, like vines, seek you
and you, your arms, sought mine.

We could have lived endlessly in those dreams.

I wanted to be every place with you, Mãe,
every place, I wanted to be with you,
and you reached out like parts of me
were made for you, so completely,
like I was me for you,
your dreams absorbing mine.
A window of light bathed us where we sat,
my back to you, your back against the couch,
my fingers twisting carpet fuzz
while yours worked, twisting, straining my oiled scalp,
and Vovó called you
(you too were a daughter first)
I heard her ask, Is my Flor there?
as if I too belonged to her.

She's out, you said,
and I could hear the voice from
between your cheek and shoulder,
the voice that would claim me and hurt you at once.
That's your brother—
like João Bosco on the guitar, you hear him?
He visits me. My daughters forget me, but he visits me.
The same brother, the same one.

I know from dreams that you cannot forget,
that my *Vovó* misunderstands or lies.
In nightmares, the bullwhip
you buried in her garden
resurrects itself back to her old work,
or else the metal end of hose
is breaking skin.
In the dreams, you want it, home,
you run from it,
you seek out crowds,
you seek the sea, alone,
though you must see me.
What am I, a shadow, you?
Am I the doubling in your dreams?
You tell me without telling me, Mãe.
I feel the sting of salt on your scraped knees.
I feel the switch where the scars will form.
I hear you muttering a need for a love

that imprints by mutilation.

My grandmother was young.
I am not nearly as young as she,
when she started with children,
when men started to take her for themselves.
My mother was younger still with taking,
but my *Vovó* was young.

At first, it was the countryside,
the red tiled roofing echoed across the valley,
and she, an echo of a dozen faces, child in a house of children,
my grandmother. She made her own story,
met and loved, close to home, an older man—
and she, in love or something else, had two children by the man
who had children with younger women still and left my
grandmother for good.
When my grandparents met,
my grandfather had left a similar village
and was never going back, and
my grandmother might follow.
And she, to get away,
had only to make one sacrifice—
a sacrifice to please the gods—
of two young children.
He would let nothing hold him back, my grandfather,

not two children from another man, not the rumors that might
follow, not the weight that would keep him in yet another village
like the one he'd left behind.
A clean break,
one son left with parents,
one son left with neighbors, they were willing,
a sacred vow of silence,
and the two were free.

The ocean is everywhere, a current for
clandestine returns to home,
secret affairs with men on boats—
my grandparents had six children besides,
and each of them took milk
intended for their brothers.
Each new child was a leech,
possessive and ungrateful,
taking blood with the milk
and crying out in agony when refused.
They want everything from her. They will kill her.

This is how children become monsters,
by monstrous mothers in haunted houses.
This is every house.

"Mãe?"
Hm?
"I don't like this story."
In the moonlight, your teeth seem to reflect blood,
seem to sharpen behind your lips.
I check my own teeth with my tongue,
but I don't feel them cutting.

Oh Flor, I'm sorry, Flor, oh, I'm sorry, sorry—
you rock me, rock yourself while holding me.
I know this story must end well,
but the telling makes you sick, makes you sleep.
I'm not afraid, I tell myself, but this story hides a riptide.
I'd be stupid not to be afraid. Stupid girl.

I tried to hide,
surrounded by water,
the water of this whole earth,
the ocean, inland,
mountains valleys canyons fields
when all I see in all directions are dry yellow grasses,
there I am, the sea keeping tabs, the ocean finding me.

"Are we going somewhere?"
"Is that why you came here?
It was you who sought me,
not the other way around."
I'm not sure I believe her.
"I don't believe you."
I'm not sure I believe Yemanjá as
she moves the water like she's
conjuring whirlpools to keep me,
to hold me between coasts.
Two coasts appear, impossibly,
on either side of the horizon.
As I scramble to an edge and grab hold,
my nails leave scratches
in the wooden raft.
My mother whispers in my ear,
calms me.
Hmmm...
Yemanjá sends little

teasing tongues of water
over the edges of the raft,
just the edges,
and we move no closer
to either coast,
my hand to my belly.
Mãe sits on the other side,
her fingers swirling the water,
patient.

I want you to be happy.
Are you still afraid?
"No."
Maybe this was true.
Do you still mourn for me?
"Yes."

Sometimes you become water—
isn't that what you've always been becoming?
You slip down the drain when no one's around,
but I know where to go to look for you,
to trace pipes, main lines, to seek you.
A girl? you ask.
The water never floods the boat, only licks it.
"What are you still doing here?"
I imagine a doctor with no face, just a voice

that says I'll have a girl, It's a girl,
a memory or a vision,
I'm determined not to let your judgments color mine.
I hope it's a girl, you say.
But you look afraid, like this possibility scares you.
"I won't be like you."
You will. It's the only way.
I wonder if this isn't all a dream,
if you've dreamed me a whole life without you
before leaving.

We were sitting there, Mãe,
in the twilight, under the imposing magnolia tree,
its roots spread like fingers upturned beneath us,
holding us,
and you turned to me.
You said nothing, only turned to me,
and I thought I could keep you there, with me, forever.

Living is only questions, Flor,
how to leave a haunted house
not trailing ghosts.
How I could live with myself,
giving you my past. How I could
look at you with the ghosts all around us.
To love you, knowing what it gave you.

And keep loving you, even with everything.
Sometimes it's impossible to live with so many ghosts.

Do you remember how we used to sit and talk
without speaking?
"How do I know I ever understood you,
what you were telling me?
How do I know I wasn't putting words in your eyes?"
You understood.
The only time you ever misunderstood
was when I made my thoughts unreachable,
when I was hiding something from you,
when my eyes lied.
"Even from me?"
"What?"
Yemanjá looks at me with the infinite eyes of the sea.
"Mãe shared everything with me,
but still she had secrets.
I thought she shared everything."
"Of course not. You were a child."
"I was so angry with her, after."
The water rolls steadily on.
"You were grieving."
"Yes, but I was also furious.
I was unforgiving.
I'm still not sure that I've forgiven her.
We were one.

She took away what was
mine, a part of me, my own, when she left."

Come into the water. Float in it.

Here you are now, whole, the way I remember you.
I remember you.
You were never fully mine
the way a daughter always dreams her mother to be,
but I remember you.

Vovó said, You are descended
from Africans and natives, and you have
inherited multitudes, magic, ghosts.
And her scales shone in moonlight
in a kitchen without a roof,
I was wary and wanting, Mãe,
like you, watching her
until all the past, history, collapsed
and my heart was a little fish, it swam to her.
Even as her scales were cutting,
sharp-edged and bloody.
Afterwards, I never wanted to go back there,
not because of what I saw in her,
but because of what I saw in me.

Do you know what I mean?
Yes.
She too was in me.
Yes.
But it was more than that.
Yes. Our pasts are inescapable.
We inherit everything.
Yes.

I remember things I could not see then.
Yes, that is the way.
I have heard things again that I could not hear then.
Yes, that is the way.
Woman after woman after woman, loving each other,
suffering, and defending each other.
Did my mother also dream her mother's dreams?
This thing must be passed down,
must be ancient.
It's not a blessing
to know your mother's pain.
It's a curse.
A child shouldn't know
that her mother regrets her.
A mother should have privacy
in those thoughts, should be able
to regret to herself, alone,
in the privacy of her own mind.

But maybe it wasn't that,
the dreaming. My grandmother
might not have wanted privacy,
might have preferred to broadcast herself,
the anger she was supposed to hide.
We are asked to hide so much, too much,
all of us.
My grandmother had eight children!
She must have only ever been having children,
raising children,
leaving children.

I want the feeling I used to have when
I'd go out to explore the yard,
always the same landscape,
a yard infinite and small at once,
but each time I found some new magic there.
I was an explorer,
noting how animals made homes of almost nothing,
an old piece of plywood in the grass.
Once, when it was raining,
I found a salamander
swimming in a puddle beside the shed.
It must have come a long way,
from some faraway pond,
leaving only when the rain started.
Usually, a body like that,

made of water, would dry up on such a journey,
across the cracked earth, the sun.
After the rain, I imagined,
its new home would evaporate, would disappear
along with its slippery body, but in that moment,
it had made a new home in the rain
where nothing had existed that morning.
I remember wondering
if the salamander knew something I didn't,
like maybe it would rain forever,
and our yard was transforming into something else entirely,
something wet,
or if moving was an impulse,
or if this was some other kind of sign for a future
I should have understood.
The salamander and the water disappeared
after the rain stopped.

"What is it you want?
Why did you come here?"
Why. Why. Why.
You wouldn't understand that answer,
the living of that answer, you wouldn't want it.
The tongues of water become her fingers on the edge of the raft.
You wouldn't want to.
You don't want to know that.
She's right. I know that she's right.

I want to un-ask. I want to go back to before I asked.
What it would take—
"Please, stop."

The sound of the ocean,
not where it crashes against the shore,
fussing into land,
but way out in the middle:
much longer swells, deliberate, deep breaths,
the wind, mostly making sound against my edges,
wind through the tunnels of my ears,
alive with sound because I am bodily,
occasionally, the splash of a fish,
an ocean breath shooting up
from below, water and air.

I consider what it means to disappear.
To disappear into a dream
is to glimpse death.
Chemicals for paralysis,
the body does this to itself—
or the brain does this to the body,
the brain, which lives most vividly
in this small death,
creates entire worlds,
renders a new body,

gives it impossible possibilities of movement.
In sleep, the mind becomes god of its universe.
People pray to die in sleep,
to disappear into it.
Sometimes you've become a dream,
your body stilled,
your mind more alive than it's ever been.
All I have to do is find you and wake you.

"Am I a girl or a dream of a girl?"
"What do you mean?"
"I don't know what I mean."

You can see me with your eyes closed.
I can.
How can you tell, when we're in bed,
every time I open my eyes?
I am your mother, your mamãe.
I just know it. I can feel it.
Does it stay with you in death?
Does it expand? Can you see me even now?

What were you dreaming, Flor?
"I was dreaming of an enormous bird
that became smaller and smaller in the sky,

and you were a little turtle becoming larger and larger
as I waited to catch you."
You didn't say you were waiting to catch me.
You told me I was a turtle, falling.
"Didn't I? This time I knew exactly where you'd fall.
All the animals had gathered,
to watch and wait for you, limbs outstretched.
It was some other animal who had caused them trouble,
a misunderstanding,
some animal from deep in the river,
not you, who hugged the riverside,
who bathed on logs and stones.
Wasn't this the world we made?
Hadn't we made a village that would believe you?
Filled with arms that would wait to catch you?
The others are gathered still, or again,
a new convening, for a new holding.
I could stand not knowing,
I could stand twisting, weaving,
making myself dizzy with my eyes on the sky, forever.
Even now, I look up to the sky and spread my arms,
waiting, watching for you."

"How did you get here? Did
you come here for a man? Did
you come here running from a man?"
The anchor at the bottom of this float

that keeps us moored in place
must have come from your steady, heavy eyes.
Did I not bring you okra seeds and dried beans
in my hair, like in the old stories?
Did I not make you pancakes of tapioca in the morning,
and breads of mandioca in the afternoon?
I came here for you.
I hoped to bring my land to foreign land in you.
"You came here also for yourself."
It's the same.
Blood that won't believe me
is blood that won't believe you.

The trees here stand alone.
One tree stretching out in
a sea of tall grasses.

You, too, have now borne alone what no body
should have to bear alone. I became human
bearing what I could not, alone. But then you came,
from the waters of the whole earth, from blood,
to make me part of history,
gift me survival, a little longer.

Mothers are always watching. Have you
noticed that? Mothers can watch
from anywhere. I would be in another room
and Mãe would call to me. I'd be far away,
unaware of my own thoughts,
and she would call me over—
What's wrong?
"Nothing."
Then she would watch me.
You're sick, Flor.
"No."
There was no time to be sick.
Your eyes are sick.
"I'm fine."
Mães don't get sick. Come lie down.
I lay down against her chest.
The fever in my head,
pulling me towards sleep
and fever dreams
filled with brambles, vines, tails
that came from me and found her,
made her sick,
made her sicker.

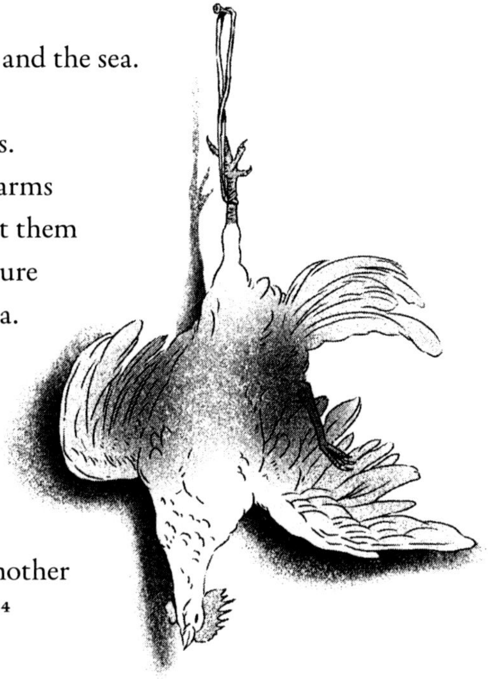

Mãe floated in the sea.
There was nothing between her and the sea.
I tried to stretch my arms to her
but there were waves between us.
I tried to reach for her with my arms
but I could not find where to put them
to touch her. I wanted to make sure
she had not dissolved into the sea.

"You are Yemanjá,
you can render ghosts."
"No, not the way you think."
"I remember one morning my mother
thought she saw a dead chicken[24]
in the clouds, *galinha morta*,
and she wouldn't go out all day.
There's a dark magic,
to bring back the dead.
There must be curses, and magic—
I'm here, aren't I? How did I get here?"
"There are no chants to resurrect the living.
There's no way for the living to survive intact."
"And the ghosts?"
"The ghosts become a need.
They become something different
from what they were before."

"How did we get here?"
You know the history we carry.
"No?"
You must always carry the history,
every story you know.
The ghosts will follow you
even if you forget.
It's better to remember.
It's better to remember.
Every ghost is where we come from.

The living, too, are becoming
something different.
Where did you go, Mãe?
After my uncle became a log,
became waterlogged driftwood,
became a ghost on the horizon,
his skin puffed up with need,
became our ghost?
The living, you can keep away,
put oceans between you and them,
but a ghost is forever.
It was the end of everything
when my uncle died,
but not in the ways we'd imagined.

The history, you mustn't forget it.
"What history? What is this really about?"
You mustn't forget it.
"I won't, see, I'm using history to tell this story:
We carried the shackles ourselves.
We put ourselves on a ship.
We locked ourselves away.
We locked even the windows."
You're being cruel. This isn't how it happened.

Are you glad I did this to myself?
"Why would you ask me that?"
This is your dream—you tell me.
"But my dreams were never my own.
I haven't dreamed since you left.
Until this, until this fruit expanding.
Now, again, I'm not myself alone,
I'm a part of two."
A ghost is forever.
"I never wanted this.
How could I be glad?"
Never?
"Why are you asking me this?"
I'm so hungry...
"Let me hold you, Mãe.
Come up from the sea so I can put my arms
around you. Put your hands here, on this float.

Let me see your wrists.
You must have cut them against some shell.
Are they better now?"

I wanted to dream about you, Mãe,
after you were gone, to remember you.
I couldn't even dream about you.
Were any of my dreams my own?
Was there not a single one?
A girl who is lost wants only to dream about her mother...

When you reach your hand into the sea and pull up a fish,
I see my grandmother in you.
I see her in both of us.
I'm hungry, too.
I hunger for anything, everything.
I'm starving.
I might kill the dolphin, swirling,
confused, in the water there,
with a sharpened stone.
I might eat him, too.
I might kill him.

"Mãe, I thought you had dissolved into the sea.
I thought you had become water."

No.
"Or that water had become blood, and flowed into you?"
Who knows what blood has become water,
and what water blood?
"I prefer water becoming blood, and then
changing into you. Is that the way you
return to me in this world, and outside of it?"
Don't you remember the story?
You must remember.
"No, I— I've forgotten."
Then she said words that I did not understand,
that I could not speak or write down.
Words that were lost to me.

The ocean is ancestral, this whole ocean.
This is family. This is in you. The ocean
is where you hold a child inside you.
The ocean is the whole story.

If you could have been my mother—
"A daughter shouldn't have to be also a mother.
I shouldn't have had to care for you that way."
I know, that's not what I meant.
I only wish she had been more like you.
It would have been so much easier.
"I dreamed of you, Mãe, did you see it?

I dreamed that you were on my breast,
and your sharp teeth cut me open."
That isn't what I meant...
"Your teeth now, the way they shine,
they look sharp. They shouldn't be so sharp.
It isn't natural.

Why are your teeth that way?"
I left all my teeth in Salvador,
all my baby teeth. I buried them.
These are the ones that grew back.
"In the dream, you drank the blood,
since there was no milk.
You drained it from both breasts, the blood."
I never meant to hurt you,
but you came from the hurt of me.
You came from it.

"Why did you do that to yourself?"
You won't understand.
"I know everything about you. How would I not understand?"
I hope that I have raised you so that you would never understand
why a woman would do this to herself.
That is my hope.
That you will never understand why I've done this.

My grandmother said it is not easy
to raise daughters in a world such as this one.
It is not easy for a mother or a daughter.
But she did not see the way
we were when she said those things.
It is not difficult to be yours in any time.

Avó told me of a river named for an elder, Uatu,
and a distant river Yuma, called a mother, that she'd heard of once,
and how to see rivers in relation,
rivers as bodies,
that rivers need tending, she told me.
A dam was built in the elder river.
The dam was supposed to be for all,
but it hurt many. Water is not a resource,
my grandmother told me, it is ancient
and sacred, to be cared for.
When the dam broke, Uatu was contaminated.

The river that was history, the river that was life
and family, poisoned all the way down.
This is what happens with dams, she told me.
When the dam is built,
consider your home already poisoned.
This, before my grandmother's body filled with cancer
and she stopped calling.

Mãe shows me where I need her,
the place where a silver thread
leaves me and connects to her,
a changing place.
It's here, she says,
tension beneath the skin of my palm
where she pulls.
Another day, *It's here.*
Our bodies make a T where she lies at my feet,
pulling thread from between my toes.
She pulls at her own chest, at her belly.
I can feel the way it tugs from her,
the way she holds multitudes,
magic in her stretch marks,
puckered trails of shooting stars and
her belly, the night.

"Ours is such a small story, Mãe,

I've been working hard to forget it. I've forgotten it."
Don't say that.
"It's a story of you and me and loss. I want to lose it.
There's no history about this story."
Of course there is.
Ours is all of history.
Ours is in the history of bodies,
of being disappeared,
of women
here and there, then and now,
of bodies, of water.
Today, the Guarani are killing for loss of land.
The Guarani are killing themselves over it,
children even.
Today is history.
Did you not also go through it? The rite of passage?
Did you not also want to kill the dolphin there?
Women are born at war. Women are soldiers.
You were too young for me to teach you these things
before, but you ought to know them by now.
The disappeared, they know it, the women and girls
who have been taken, and the ones from whom
much has been taken besides.
Ours is a story among many stories
that should not be forgotten.
Ours is a history, a testament against forgetting.
You were born here,
You were born in the water

across this whole earth, descended
from African women and Native women,
from every woman,
from woman at war.

"I'm here because you brought me here.
I was born here."
We come from others who went through
what we went through,
and others who went through,
and others.

You came to me from endless days
soaking on the beach,
from hiding myself
in the sounds of the Farol da Barra[25]
You must be made of the belly of the drum,
of ocean mist.
When I carried you,
I'd fall asleep beside the speakers at home
and feel you dance in me,
an amniotic jongo.[26]

The windy roar to life, the sea, refrain.
The ocean is a rhythm.

25 A fort made by the Portuguese, a replacement lighthouse "gifted" by the British. It's difficult to hear anything amongst the raucous energy here, the competing music from coastal facing bars, the group of drummers that comes to perform. If you look out across the bay, and you're listening beyond the noise, you can feel the voices of resistance coming off the island of Itaparíca, the battles led by black and Tupinambá and Tapuia women for Brazilian independence. Their phantom battle cries are louder than anything if you know what to listen for.

26 Another in a long list of traditions with Afro-Brazilian roots. A dance.

When I press my cheek to Mãe's chest,
I can hear the rhythm of the ocean inside of her.
I wonder if I sound the same.
My hair across my face,
the feel of seaweed,
sticky with the salty air.
My mother is from and of oceans.

"When you are remembering,
your memories peel off
you like skin, your body, selves.
I am afraid for you then.
I keep seeing flashes of you, on the ceiling,
in the corners, in the doorway,
like pieces of you escape you.
And then what comes back?
your arms, your love like a need.
I am reborn in that need, Mãe,
and you open new."
She splashes, says nothing, while I speak
of discovery, of survival by moving through.
We change shape, we are not reborn, she says.
Her eyes on me.

"What is the relation between history and place?
What if I had said,

'This isn't the place for me, Mãe'?
But place finds you in spite of leaving."
Her eyes, glowing, watching.
"I saw your memories, Mãe."
I didn't mean for you to see them.
I wanted to raise you without your knowing them.
But ghosts seek you and you can't
hide from them, even across an ocean.
I wanted to be new with you,
to come to you without those memories.
"I wanted to hold you to me, Mãe.
I wanted to make it so that the memories
would stop coming, would disappear.
Would be forgotten
somewhere they couldn't be found. I wanted to
pull all the memories. Or take them and swallow them
if that would make them go away. They were
bitter, rotting memories, but I would have swallowed them
whole, if I thought that they would die inside me.
But history and place won't stop coming,
moving in like dark clouds to this place and this time.
Do you think a day will come
when mothers with daughters will forget the stories,
will have no need for them?
Do you think so in this world?
And then the day when the warring would be over,
the sea would open and drown the memories,
would leave only birth.

And those who know how to tell new stories,
and how even to sharpen stories against spirits,
would forget that knowledge.
They wouldn't remember it anymore."
She doesn't answer.
She disappears.

I've forgotten the stone.
The stone is a small, sharp thing now,
nothing, cutting into my palm.
I'm alone, on an enchanted boat,
not sure if I'm coming or going.
You won't be like me, Mãe says into my ear,
her voice alone, without a body.
I was wrong. You won't be like me.
You are not so close to me that we share everything.
We are not the same.

In Salvador, my grandmother tells me to come close.
"Sit here," she says.
"You love me."
It sounds like a set of instructions: Sit here, you, love me.
The house has been filled with the yelping
of a dozen small dogs all morning,
my grandmother's voice cutting through theirs,
Cala a boca, shut up!

"Not your mother," *Vovó* is saying.
"She remembers nothing good about me."
Something was in her hands,
a necklace she was putting together with seeds,
a gift for me, on the table now.
"She remembers like I never did anything for her."
My mother's dreams are in the room with us,
as my grandmother pulls me closer,
shaking me by the shoulders a little as she holds me,

I think,
or maybe I've imagined the shaking.
I can't understand exactly what is happening, the words,
the way the memories I've seen in dreams are changing shape.
I question even the memories.
I have seen them myself, and I question them.

In a room in my mind, a water stain
creeps down the painted plaster.
I imagine the entire wall becoming a shade darker,
and no one to notice.
My hair gets longer, goes unwashed, knots,
loses the burgundy of the sun,
deepens to the color of deep sea,
nobody to ask what seeks shelter there
in the wilds, ocean bottom, my scalp, a world.

My hair, like the afros of my ancestors, holds multitudes.
My hair could save us both, or drown us.

When my mother shaves her head,
she seems to find new life.
She can feel the breeze dance across her scalp
in all new ways.
She can feel the sea inside and out.
She feels herself unleashed.

The mane of Yemanjá must be seaweed
alive at the roots.

My mother, drowning.
My mother, disappearing herself
into the sea within without.
My mother, poetry alive, the deep sea.

What did you come here for?
I wanted you to be ok.
I wanted to find you and to be enough for you.
It was never a question of you being enough.
You were everything,
but no one could change what had already happened.

Another person, any human being, even I, myself,
I could not have changed the past.
No matter how many times I brought you into my past—
my past to you.
Then why did you bring me inside?
At first I didn't even know I was doing it.
You were there, and you were me.
Or I thought that you were me.
You felt so absolutely mine,
I didn't even see you as you,
in my dreams.
And then I saw you—I remember the first time,
it was at the caves, on the shoreline,
the memory of my secret escape.
The sun was making me sweat,
the light was reflecting off my skin in the magic of dreams.
I was dazzled by it, the fracturing of light off my own skin,
I turned my arm one way, another,
and there, that's where I saw your skin beneath mine,
or your arm over mine, or—
you were there. That's when I saw you.
And you were witnessing me.
My shame, my rage, my fear,
you witnessed memories that were only mine.
It felt good for someone to see me
in a way I had never been seen.
I thought, this is motherhood.
This is the gift.

You see me.
It isn't though, Mãe—motherhood isn't that.
That's something else.
There are boundaries, limits.
We had something beyond language, but with all of that,
with all that we had, made, it wasn't enough.
Why couldn't it be enough?
That was never the point of it.
I only ever needed you to see me.

I don't want to forget you.
Then don't. Tell the story to others.
You will tell the story, and in it, I will be a god.
I will be all the animals in the stories I taught you.
I will be the cracked dirt of the earth.
You will tell the story of how you came to me,
and I will be yours, more and more each time.

Here now, we near a bay, an island,
people moving along the coastline,
a mirage, a painting, a dream.
The rhythms become louder,
but they are not new. I am new.
I am new to the rhythms with no end
and no beginning.
I cannot see Yemanjá,

but the water of the bay
feels a part of her,
from her.
I, myself, of and from her,
I still feel her in me.
The beat continues, the rhythm
of dreaming and waking, both.

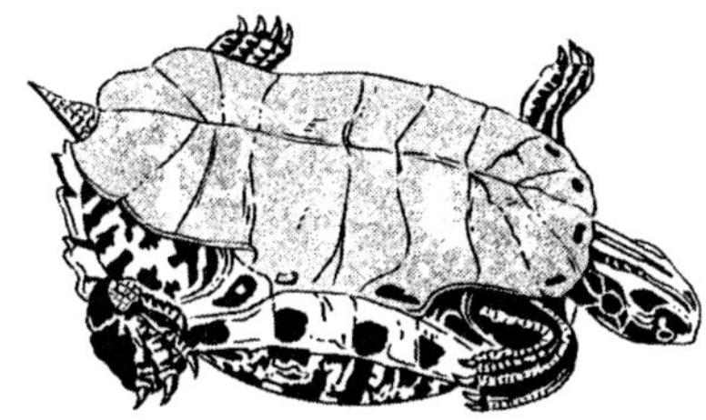

II

We come from the west coast of Africa,
from women transported on boats,
from home,
from lost bloodlines, from monsters with
bottomless bellies,
from the West Indies, conquest, uprisings,
revolution, and bloodshed—
We come from warrior women
on all sides.

Sou de Nanã, euá. Euá, euá, ê
Sou de Nanã, euá. Euá, euá, ê [27]

27 From a slave song, *Cordeiro de Nanã*, the lyrics are “I am of Nanã.” *“Euá, euá, ê”* is just sound, a feeling in syllables, melancholia. *Nanã*, in Candomblé, is the goddess who created the universe. The music is sweet, but the words tell of slavery, of how the singer was called a sheep of *Nanã* but retained something valuable in his choice to remain quiet rather than speak and be told no. The words ask for a moment of silence for the senseless suffering created in the slavery which the singer has endured.

We come from the kingdom of warrior
women on the left banks of the Amazon.
Caité, the full moon, brings longing.
She pulls the tides within us until
all we are is need.
Even we, the warriors, are moved.

“What do you know of the stories
that were never taught to you?”
It is not a question when Yemanjá asks,
playfulness in her eyes like pools at low tide,
children splashing, reflection of the setting
sun, a game, a challenge, a new script,
the eulogy a song we are writing together.
“They’ve come to me a dozen
different ways.
I learned them in the *aviso* of the *roda*,
the songs of the *vagabundo*,
forbidden traditions of the poor.
The essence and ancestry on the
string of the *berimbao* and the
throb of the *atabaque*,
the words rising up on many voices.[28]

28 The traditions of *capoeira* are rooted not only in its dance-like fighting style but in story. Every song, every *aviso*, tells a story both by language and rhythm. Like all old storytelling traditions, the people assemble for the roda in a circle and participate actively in the telling. The *berimbao* and the *atabaque* keep time. The songs tell the kinds of histories that have been kept hidden, the kinds that get its practitioners labeled as vagabonds and miscreants, the kinds that have even gotten capoeira outlawed at different points in Brazil’s not so long ago history.

Que navio é esse
que chegou agora
é o navio negreiro
com os escravos de Angola
aqui chegando
não perderam a sua fé
criaram o samba
a capoeira e o candomblé.[29]

Among the enslaved arriving by boat,
I see my mother's eyes
that well with waves, the sea,
and I, myself, am the *axé*,
by sea, the eyes,
the samba, *capoeira*, candomblé.

"In the old stories, the stories outside time,
before time,
the stories used to teach us how to tell stories,
there you are."
"How?"
I want to test her in return, to hear the words as waves again.
"What explanation is there for that
which has no explanation?
Do I need to explain everything to you?

29 From the *capoeira* song *O Navio Negreiro*, the rhythm haunts you. It enters into your dreams. It becomes one of the rhythms to which your life moves. "What ship is this / that has just arrived / it's the slave ship / with the slaves of Angola / coming here / they did not lose their faith / they created samba / capoeira and candomblé."

The tide recedes, and there lie bodies.
The blood is in the earth, unforgetting.
In the earth, the blood
of the dead tells stories.
There you are."
"Yes..."
"There you are."

In the battle for independence,
on the island of Itaparica,
off the coast of Salvador,
in the Bay of All Saints,
a Bahia de Todos os Santos,
my mother, *com as afro-brasileiras,*
as Tupinambás, as Tapuias,[30]
minha mãe.

The legacy of women warriors is
the fisherman's knife,
the poisonous *cansancão* plant,
the fires set to ships and bodies
of men stripped naked, seduced and killed.

30 It is said that on the island of Itaparica, a group made up largely of black and indigenous women fought a critical battle in the Brazilian struggle for independence. They were instructed to evacuate the island for their safety, but they chose to stand their ground.

My mother is Maria Felipa,
on the island,
leading me into battle
and an army of women.
My mother leading every battle,
Joana Angélica shouting
from the mainland too,
You will only get in over my dead body!
She thrusts her body before a cloister,
standing on legs spread wide
as if she might birth the future of Brazil
as she fights for my escape.

In Palmares, in another time, Dandara,
story lost and legend both, leader and defender,
Dandara planting, hunting, fighting
to be free, that is the way here, my mother
learns and teaches,
that is the way here.
A *luta*, the fight,
preparing for battle even as she dances,
a *luta*, in all parts of life,
that is the way.

"Do you know the stories before time,
in the beginning?
In the beginning, Moon desires.
Moon meets Sun in the Amazon
before there are oceans,
before there are rivers,
before there is water across the whole earth,
Sun meets Moon beneath a canopy of trees, and
there are no words yet for what one feels for the other."

Moon dreams are apocalyptic.
When Moon dreams of love,
the earth goes up in flames and floods,
Moon's tears of consummation
flood the whole earth

as Sun cries out, *Jaci, Jaci.* Sun, overcome,
whose flames desire, *Jaci...* the Sun sets
all of earth ablaze when Moon dreams.

"Yes, I know the stories.
There, in the beginning, Moon brings longing:
controlled tears of loss
are not the wild wailings of passion.
Apart from the Sun, Moon does not flood the universe,
only drops tears on the forests, in the valleys,
her tears become the oceans, the rivers and lakes,
Moon mourns, alone, and life on earth goes on.
But the waters of *saudade* are the womb
which births us all, in the beginning,
the reason Moon holds the sea, the tides in us."

There is no night, in the beginning.
My mother commands the night.
One animal gazes into the eyes of another to create life,
and there is my mother in the Tupi tale,
daughter of the sea snake,
calling.

The coconut holds night,
holds First Night sounds,

crickets and toads,
siren sounds of first night,
and mere men to deliver it.

In every story the animals transform,
the basket holding night becomes a wild cat,
the disobedient men become monkeys, and
I, night released, my mother desperate to contain me—

My mother is in the animals, too,
the *Onça*, from so many of the old tales,
the jaguar, my mother.
She is strong, but always hungry.
The other beasts trick her often.
I see her at one end of a hollow tree trunk
while at the other end, turtle slinks away.
Monkey laughs.
My mother starves.
She is cut open.

They make a fire and dance around her corpse.
My mother is an offering.
My mother becomes earth.
Even her vibrant coat dissolves into dust.
Every animal dissolves.

The land is fertile with bodies.

In the old stories, my mother is the *Onça*
who wants too much, everything,
who wants to learn the magic,
who begs and begs and begs and begs,
and gets her eyes eaten by fish.
There is magic all around her,
but no one will teach her.
Crab uses magic to disappear her eyes,
Buzzard uses magic to make her new ones.
Monstrous *Curupira* uses magic to help man hunt her down.

My mother is all the *Onças*,
whose bones are the measure of a warrior's strength,
who learns to cry while running,
whose tears become stains,
who mourns always, to the melodies of the flutes
made from other *onça* bones.

"Do you only know stories of jaguars, *menina?*"
Yemanjá's laugh is a steady hum,
the imitation echo in a seashell
"I know only stories of my mother."
"Yes, she is in all the stories.

She is and you are, both."
And because I am just getting warmed up
I say, "We are *onça* in the stories,
we are monkey too.
We are stars who once were black birds,
we are even *Jabutí*."
"The turtle! Tell me the story this way."
So I do, I give her retellings of retellings of retellings...

"When Mãe is *Jabutí*, it is *Onça* causing trouble,
running after sun for a fire to cook by.
My mother wants only to eat what she has hunted.
She eats the meat raw, little turtle, while *Onça* is away."

My mother, the turtle, is trapped high in a tree.
She throws the fruit down to insatiable *Onça*.
Desperate, she tosses herself from the tree,
she makes herself a weapon.
In this way, she kills the *Onça*.

The turtle likes trouble, but she is also clever.
She makes a flute of *Onça's* bones
to sing her songs of conquest.
She attracts other jaguars.

She tricks them all.
My mother survives.
Her shell breaks into a dozen pieces when she falls,
but she survives a long time.

Mãe is a legend
told for lessons at bedtime.
"Have you heard the story of…?"
"Yes, I know it.
I know her by the stories.
She shared them all."

The *Curupira*, protector of the Amazon, capable of magic,
who runs ahead on backward facing feet,
who knows how to lose men in the woods,
who knows how to keep them.
She is ugly and bald, with colored teeth and pointed ears.
She is strong. She is angry.
She is the whistle of wind, night noises, false tracks,
keeper of trees, vengeance of the Amazon.
My mother is true to her word.

She is a nightmare, my mother,
the horrifying *Kibungo*, the beast of Bahia.
The opening in her back is a mouth, which opens wide
and swallows whole. My mother hungers, always.

Villagers throw boiling water on her legs,
they stab her in the neck,
they beat her.
She swallows up their children,
and they chase her away.
Nobody asks her what she wants,
or what she needs,
or why she eats.
My mother is afraid,
and she is lonely,
she is hungry.
She does not die.
She does not die.
She's coming back,
they chant, they sing.
Kibungo will be back.

When the girl, my mother,
goes wandering at night,
my mother, *Kibungo*, consumes her.

And when the girl, my mother, calls out for help
in the old stories, no one can save her.
She disappears into *Kibungo*,
and only *Kibungo* is left.

"Do you know the *carranca*?"
"The ugly faces carved on boats,
Haunting the Rio São Francisco,
she is clever, my mother,
to make herself this way,
floating along the rivers, back and forth,
the scowling guardian of men."

She keeps the evil river spirits at bay,
and fights with a look, a *luta*.
Because she is frightening
she survives.
She is many ugly faces.
It is safer this way.
It is safer to be an ugly mask
than it is to be a woman.
It is better to be wood making
the same journeys,
back and forth, wearing smooth
in the waters with time.

In the old stores of the Sataré-Mawé,
my mother is a woman
tricked by mother after mother after mother.
They tell her lies about their sons.
She is surrounded by jealous brothers
in the enchanted garden of Noçoquem
who want her only to themselves.
Cursed by knowledge,
she marries a hawk.
She marries a snake.
She births my brother.
She tells him all the stories.
She births my brother, who in death becomes the manioc root,
who in death becomes a tree.
The guaraná comes from my brother's right eye
after his uncles kill him,
when his body is buried deep in the ground and watered
my brother is the fruit tree that grows from the same spot.

In the old stories, even the young Bororo boys become violent.
their desire breeds rage,
their rage breeds fear,
their eyes become stars,
their women become cats, wild and howling.

The Bororo boys want the food made only for men.

They force the old woman to make it for them,
then cut out her tongue so she cannot speak.
They kill her.
They are boys and my mother,
the old woman who makes it for them,
the same one whose tongue they cut out.
As a woman, my mother tells the stories to her lover,
and everyone dies. She prays to the moon.
Vitoria Regia, the giant water lily,
blooms wide and white across the river
from the body of her dead lover.
There I am, in the darkness,
in the water below its sprawling leaves.

"With you, your mother wants more time."
"Everyone always wants more time in the old stories.
Everyone always wants more time."

I help with her disguises.
We travel far from home
and practice the spells.
We make a new home.
We eat well.
Death comes when we are happy.
This is always the moment, in the stories,
when we've learned all the magic to live easy.
Death comes.
We try to cheat the old woman,
maybe survive awhile longer,
but death always wins out in the end.

In the village, my mother follows custom
until she doesn't, until she drops off,
until she must leave.
My mother is with the people
until they decide she is against them.
She must run a long way off,
some stories travel a long way,
to meet a talking skull.
She tries to bring the people to it

but ends up a talking skull herself.

She is in motion, in the coordinated movements
across a field, across a wood, across the hard floor
of home. My mother struggles with the group, against them.

In the stories, the storyteller leads,
and a chorus of voices lifts up to them,
my mother among the voices
but also apart from them. There is
the storyteller, the chorus, my mother.
This does not bode well for her.

In the stories my mother is possessed by the gods,
she shivers and delivers a message
that the people will not hear.
She did not ask to be a messenger,
and the people did not ask for a message.

"She is not always this way."
"No, I see her in the others, too,
in the dark-skinned woman
with many children,
cleaning houses,

another selling bags of avocados
at a busy intersection in the city,
under the beating sun,
under the moving shadow of a big tree,
and others still."

At the end of a long street,
past the windows of her neighbors,
my mother sits in a plastic chair under the *mangueira*,
under the mango tree, feeding children with bread and stories.
She is tired, aging.
She has already taught an entire village
on this island whose history is women.
She has helped them all to remember.

Now an old woman,
she tells of walking into a house where a mother
tries to make soup from a stone in boiling water.
She forgets she has already told this story,
so over and over, she gives the woman food
and teaches her to eat.

The people come up with a dozen names for
each other,
caboclo, cafuzo, mulato, and pardo,
so eager for categories, as if what we are was
ever more
than myths, than legends and folklore.
I see Mãe across time,
an inheritance of all peoples,
histories intertwining,
the moon, who moves the oceans,
Yemanjá, who bore the oceans,
the silt at the bottom of the river,
moving slowly,
Mamãe.

This is what she offers me,
that all history might be mine.
With all peoples to claim me,
I might always find my way to her—

III

Odô, axé odô, axé odô, axé odô
Odô, axé odô, axé odô, axé odô
Isso é pra te levar no ilê
Pra te lembrar do badauê
Pra te lembrar de lá [31]

To summon Yemanjá,
we wear white and blue.
We bring our drawings, statues,
representations, white roses,
perfumes, oils,
beaded necklaces, mirrors,

31 Lyrics from the song *Muito Obrigado Axé*, as sung by Maria Bethânia and Ivete Sangalo. The song uses Yoruba words throughout, like “odô” for thanks or gratitude, “axé” representing an essence, a spiritual energy, “ilê” meaning home and “badauê” a celebration of happiness. These lyrics might then translate roughly to a repetition of gratitude and “axé” in the chorus, and then, “This is to bring you home / to remind you of the ‘badauê’ / to remind you of there.”

manjar branco.[32]
This side of coastline, the stories are all
salt water and dreams, all the same
ghosts, fingers in ribs, *pedindo licença*,
dissolving into seafoam.

We are on an island surrounded by women.
This is my mother's homeland.
This is the mango tree from the stories,
the island refuge of cousins and aunties.
This is not my mother's homeland–
the women have come and gone, I am not
the only one the ocean has delivered.

"We have been waiting for you.
Take this,"
a woman takes the stone from my hand,
"leave this,"
replaces it with a necklace of seeds.

We are on an island.
I am on an island with you.
You are the waters, dancing.
I listen for music that isn't my mother's voice

32 Brazilian coconut pudding dessert

but she is in all of it, singing us forward,
singing from somewhere in me.

“It doesn’t matter
that you will make all the same mistakes
in different ways.”
A woman who is the same as me and different
reads the future in the new lines crossing my belly.
Another holds a child to her chest,
sings to her granddaughter.

Sou de Nanã, euá. Euá, euá, ê
Sou de Nanã, euá. Euá, euá, ê.

When the tide comes in,
it brings the breeze inland.
When the tide goes out,
the air is still and all I feel is
heat and moisture.

Sometimes you are a planet,
and I am your moon in orbit,
your gravity, your rivers,

you are stone I am palm
you are starfish I am night sky.

The fishermen load their boats with offerings,
the roses, sweet rice, coconut puddings,
jewelry, money.
The fishermen take the peoples' offerings
out to sea,
to deliver these dreams and wishes to Yemanjá,
to ask and give thanks.

I have made a life of memories
that don't even belong to me.
Stories living in the body,
rooted in bone marrow
same as shame
same as love.
Saltwater will not wash all of it away.
I know this, and yet.

Yemanjá presides over Saturdays,
days with nowhere to be, with time
stretching and compressing
with the movement of the shadows.
This is a homecoming and a newcoming both.

I don't know what happens next,
where we are going,
only that we are here now.

"So many questions,"
says the one with the granddaughter
gesturing with her free hand
like a bird passing by her ear and behind her.
She laughs at me but she is holding me,
as long as she holds her granddaughter
she is holding me,
I am sure of it. I hold you too.

I can't tell you if we were delivered here,
or if I brought you here myself.
I hear drumming day and night,
and the women tell me
they too are my family.
I belong to them too.
They belong to me.
They hold space for me.
They swear and dance and laugh and drink
and sleep with their windows wide open.

They too know my mother's stories.
She, I, you were never alone.
I tell them anew,
I stay up all night
murmuring stories into my cupped palms
and holding them to my belly.

The women, they change before my eyes.
The oldest one sits beneath the tree
greeting everyone by name,
becomes a child, swinging her legs
above the dirt, a little girl,
becomes smaller still, a bird,
roosts in the branches overhead,
calls many names at me because
I too change, have always been changing,
a whole life and never once the same.

Through the night, the breeze comes and goes,
the still, humid heat comes and goes.
You are being formed
in the rhythm of the drum,
in the belly of the *atabaque*,
in this body of water.

The truth is that I contain oceans.
I house history, time.
I contain oceans all my own.

The morning delivers a cooling rain
and the women tell me that the bay
is made of the tears of Yemanjá.
They tell me the story of Yemanjá,
of her children, like Oxum dressed in gold,
of her adopted twins who tricked death.
They call me by her name,
and when they do I deliver messages
to them I do not understand,
in a language I do not understand.
They sing to me.

Isso é pra te levar no ilê
Pra te lembrar do badauê
Pra te lembrar de lá

Isso é pra te levar no meu terreiro
Pra te levar no candomblé
Pra te levar no altar

Isso é pra te levar na fé
Deus é brasileiro
Muito obrigado axé [33]

I respond in new old tongues.
Odô, axé odô, axé odô, axé odô

“The spirit moves me to tell you this,”
says one woman who calls me her cousin,
who calls herself my aunt.
“Maybe it’s something you need to hear.
Your mother held a great sadness.
You have come here to resolve
what she never could.”

“A pior solidão é a dois,”
another aunt says.
The worst loneliness is in two.

Sometimes you are a blood clot,
world-ending and nothing at all.

33 “This is to bring you to my ‘terriero’ (a space where candomblé is practiced) / to bring you to candomblé / to bring you to the altar. // This is to bring you to faith / God is Brazilian / many thanks to axé”

I am still angry. Here at the end I am still un-wholed
But even this grief becomes part of me,
in it there is me—
the tired and inconsolable longing
that once clung to diaphragm and lungs has settled
down and down, into my heels.
There is you, emerging from behind a ribcage,
splitting open a closed story to be told anew.
There is an unfamiliar language of future and rest,
without whose words I have only action.
I do as the women tell me.

"Bathe in this water,"
they tell me,
"After the leaves finish steeping."
And it reminds me of the baths
that Tia Malu used to give us.
"A spirit tries to enter you.
A spirit has entered.
You don't understand,
but you will.
You don't understand what it is I say,
but you will understand.
Do not wet your head in this water."

"Here is a tea for you.
Here is the medicine."
They boil a large fruit with
green skin and white flesh,
cut and peel it,
spread it in butter.
It is starchy like a potato,
"like cassava," they tell me,
"to settle the stomach."

Sometimes you are a tiny fish
flitting around in a pool,
I dip my feet in,
you tickle my toes.

Children bathe in the mouth of a river
that meets the sea,
saltwater creatures dribble through freshwater,
seashells and the fallen leaves.

I feel I've been here before.

There is an underwater spirit who sings,
but she does not want to do us harm.

I am more tired than I have ever been.
She sings a song to deliver my sadness
to the *orixás*.
She makes me light,
weightless, floating.
I remember underwater dreams
without the long ropes of kelp
that wrap and pull.
I remember sunlight and moonlight,
light at all times of day and night, stars.
I remember that I am a part of this too.

They are teaching me to let go here.
They sing along to music I do not hear.
It isn't forgetting I should learn—
memory is as important as it ever was.
Anger, sadness, guilt, grief,
all of it to be held, shared, laid out.
They teach me the music.

...Joga as armas prá lá
Faz a festa...
...Joga as armas pra lá
Faz um samba... [34]

They sit at a plastic table outside
prepping big bags of small shrimp.
It turns their fingers pink, orange.
They make rhythms on the table,
and the rhythms say,
"Now is the time for life."

...Joga as armas prá lá
Traz a orquestra...
...Joga as armas prá lá
Faz a festa... [35]

I wonder if even they know
what they will do next.
"Tomorrow we'll eat with the *orixás*,"
as if to answer my thoughts.
"*Caruru, vatapá, acarajé,*
xinxim de galinha, canjica,
arroz, feijão, sonhos—"
The food is a poem and a prayer.
In my mind, I recite along with them
and then, when they finish their list,
I murmur the names of the foods aloud
to myself all afternoon, *vatapá, caruru,*
these words were made to be a lullaby,
sonhos, sonhos, sonhos...[36]

35 "Throw your weapons away / bring the orchestra / Throw your weapons away / throw a party"
36 *Sonhos* is the name for a Brazilian dish, but it also translates to "dreams." Dreams as a meal, as an ending, as a wish.

I sleep holding you inside me,
but I am amniotic.
There is the whole world outside,
and in here, encapsulated on this island,
I have only to grow myself, to grow the spirit.
A stone comes to mind, but I think it may have
fallen to the bottom of the sea.
It will still absorb sunlight
through the water,
waiting for its next life.

And what about you?
You who may be a daughter
or anyone?

In the morning,
the islanders arrive in the shared
space beneath the wide branches of the *mangueira*
between the houses of the women
who have taken us in.
Plastic tables appear, plastic chairs,
a man with a guitar on his back,
though the music would happen anyway.
The air fills with smells and heat from all directions,
kitchens thick with mashes of beans and roots,
with fish and meats on hot stoves.

The air fills with conversation, laughter,
singing, drumming, playing,
Havaianas slapping,
we let ourselves be lifted into a samba.
We are here.

They fill a plate for us with food,
and we, with gratitude, accept it.
We eat a dish for every orixá,
every god,
every woman,
for all peoples of all times,
we sing the songs and become one, found,
more and more with each beat, line, and verse...

Odô, axé odô, axé odô, axé odô...

Acknowledgements

This book started writing itself before I came to it, and so I am grateful for all of the stories shared with me that made it into the world of *Little Fish*, for the grandparents, aunts, uncles, cousins, and friends whose lives and hearts have touched me both directly and indirectly. I would like to express my deepest gratitude to my family for their unwavering support on this journey.

To my mother, who helped me talk through the development of *Little Fish* at every stage and was always down for late nights and a good cry. To my father, for his reading and encouragement, and for being the source of my interest in fantasy. To my brother, David, and my sisters, Erin and Natasha, for keeping me sane throughout the pandemic. To all of my readers, especially my peers, professors, and visiting writers in the UNLV MFA program, to Doug Unger, Maile Chapman, Don Revell, and Mary South. To the Lusophone crew, Flavia and Susana—I know our forays into the desert and late night conversations on rooftops were crucial to the birthing of *Little Fish*. To my partner Alex, for his curiosity and support throughout my creative process, for his adventurous spirit and hand-holding, and for letting a Brazilian auntie use magic and herbs on him for physical and spiritual healing as long as it made it into the book somehow.

To Gayl Jones for writing Song for Anninho, a book written forty years ago without which this one would've never found its footing. I want to thank Alycia Calvert for being a fierce advocate without whom I wouldn't have found this book's publisher.

A special thanks to Chris Vega, for finding me at the right place and the right time, for being such a force for good in the publishing world, and to Katharine Threat for the thoughtful edits and revision notes. Thank you to my writing mentor, Carla du Pree, who models literary community engagement for me in ways that have proven crucial to my artistic development. An especially big thank you to the women of Mar Grande, Tia Iraci, Gina, Cica, Orência, and Conça, who added so much magic and possibility to the development of Parts II and III of *Little Fish*, for their folklore, for their care, for the education they offered me, for their continued work in their community, the hidden stories they revealed, their spells, their food, and their hospitality. To the rest of the Mar Grande family, especially Mestre Jaime for offering additional cultural and historical background, and to Mirinho for taking me to see the celebrations and worship of Iemanjà. To Luciany Aparecida and Sarah Kersley whose creative work introduced me to more voices and experiences from Salvador and beyond. To Irene, for her willingness to play in the world of *Little Fish* and breathe new depths of creation into it.

I send a final thank you into the universe, to "Papai" for his mask carvings, grandparenting, and inheritances over the years, to him and all the other elders who have come and gone, to Iemenjà herself, to the ghosts and deities who continue to guide my pen, and to you, for reading.

About the Author

Sylvia Fox is a Berlin-based writer interested in folklore, mysticism, migration, histories of colonialism and the African diaspora. She grew up in Texas with family stories told in a mixture of Portuguese and English about border crossings and the passing down of trauma through generations, which she continues to explore in her creative projects. Her writing explores the intersection of oral storytelling and intergenerational immigration narratives and the influence of the transatlantic slave trade along the Brazilian coastline. Sylvia holds an MFA in Creative Writing from the University of Las Vegas, Nevada. You can find her work at ***The Acentos Review*** and ***Little Patuxent Review.***

Sylvia has also worked to support other artists and promote community engagement through the Arts and Culture sector, programming for festivals, professional development, and other event work, in addition to political advocacy. She believes in a future built by uplifting other voices, especially those historically marginalised and underrepresented.

About the Press

Blue Cactus Press is an independent and grassroots publisher. Our mission is to craft books and experiences that serve as tools to help us bridge the gap between words and action. Our books are written and made by people from historically marginalized groups.

We envision a world in which books empower & celebrate communities we walk in. We strive to implement equitable business models that center collective liberation as the rule, not the exception, and offer makers dignity, autonomy, and creative voice in our practices. We work toward a future in which our planet is prioritized over profit and publishing practices are accessible and gate-free.

We seek creatively satisfying, financially viable, and relationally resonant work. We value curiosity, craftsmanship, and relational responsibility among humans, our environment, and other living organisms.

To support the press, please request our books at libraries, become a member at patreon.com/bluecactuspress or purchase our books at bluecactuspress.com

Little Fish
by Sylvia Fox

ISBN: 979-8-9873352-9-1

First edition
Cover design, illustrations, and layout by Irene Chin
Editing by Katharine Threat

Portions of the land acknowledgement used in this book, particularly text written in the Twulshootseed language, are from the Puyallup Tribal Language Program website. The mission of this program is, "to be kind, be helpful and be sharing in terms of revitalizing the Twulshootseed language by producing language users."

Blue Cactus Press makes a monthly donation to the Puyallup Tribal Language Program as a small token of our gratitude for their use of language materials, and to show respect to the puyaləpabš, also known as the Puyallup Tribe of Indians. We thank the Puyallup Tribal Language Program and puyaləpabš for the use of this valuable resource and for access to this land.

Find out more about the Puyallup Tribal Language Program at puyalluptriballanguage.org.

Blue Cactus Press | caləłali